DUSTBIN DAD

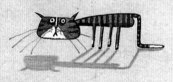

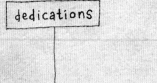
dedications

For Mum and Dad
PB
For Mum and Dad
RA

SIMON AND SCHUSTER
First published in Great Britain in 2013
by Simon and Schuster UK Ltd
1st Floor, 222 Gray's Inn Road, London WC1X 8HB
A CBS Company

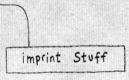
imprint stuff

Text copyright © 2013 Peter Bently
Illustrations copyright © 2013 Russell Ayto
The right of Peter Bently and Russell Ayto to be identified
as the author and illustrator of this work has been asserted
by them in accordance with the Copyright, Designs and
Patents Act, 1988
All rights reserved, including the right of reproduction in
whole or in part in any form
A CIP catalogue record for this book is available from
the British Library upon request
978-1-84738-873-5 (HB)
978-1-4711-2528-7 (PB)
978-0-85707-900-8 (eBook)
Printed in China
5 7 9 10 8 6 4

DUSTBIN DAD

title

dustbin

dad

author

PETER BENTLY

and RUSSELL AYTO

illustrator

SIMON AND SCHUSTER

London   New York   Sydney   Toronto   New Delhi

My dad is a dustbin. The one thing he hates
is seeing us leave any food on our plates.

'Don't throw it out!
It's got flavour and taste!
Just pass it to me
and it won't go to waste!'

cat's tail

So Dad gobbles up all our leftover food.
(Even the bits that are squishy and chewed.)

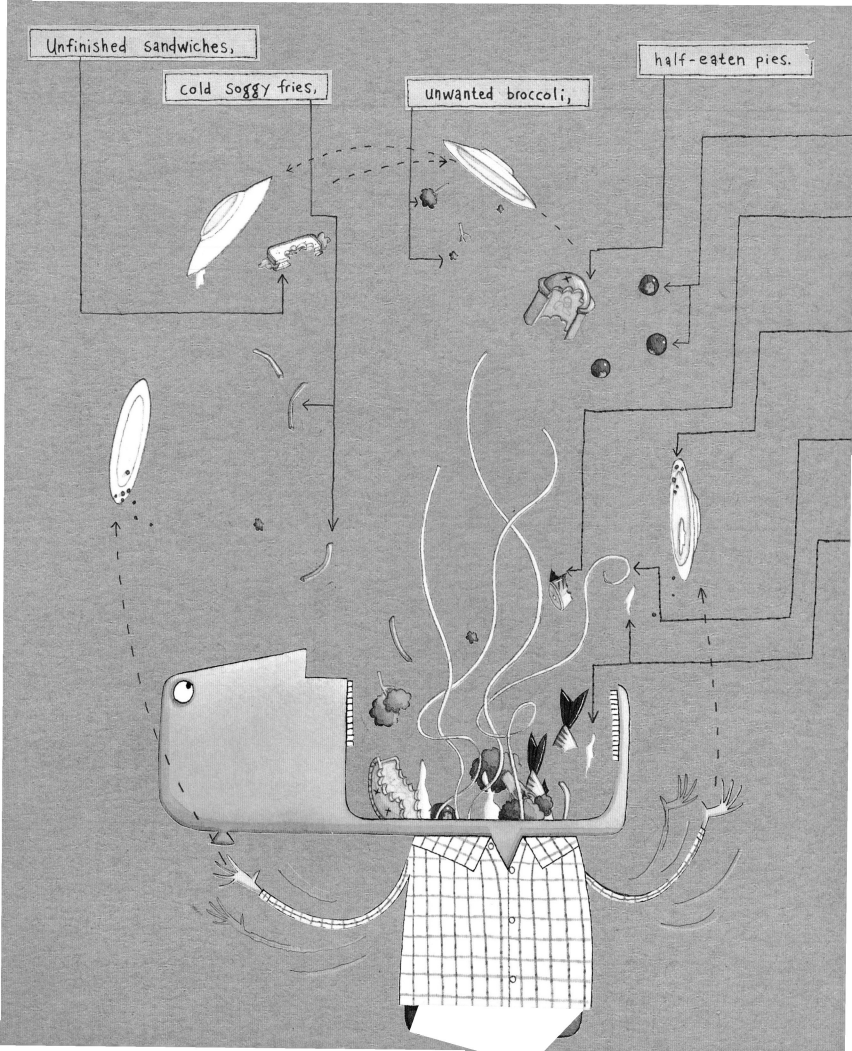

Tomatoes with toothmarks,

odd scraps of fish,

crunchy bits left on the side of the dish.

Clammy spaghetti,

the whites of boiled eggs —

'Your father,' says Mum,

'is a dustbin on legs.'

Now, we have a cat named Amelia Scrimp –
she's sweet but, quite frankly, a bit of a wimp.

'That mog,' said the vet, 'needs some Puss-Pep-Up-Powder.

You mix it with water.

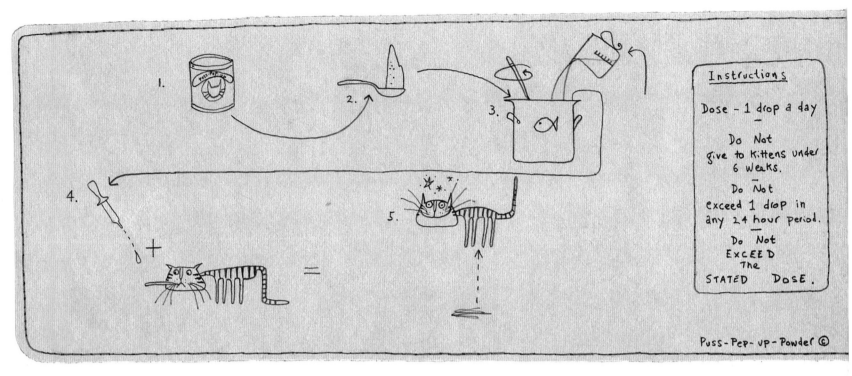

It tastes like fish chowder.

One droplet will perk up your puss-cat like heck.

Later that day, on a snack-finding snoop,
Dad saw a pot and thought, 'Leftover soup!'

He tasted one spoonful, then two, and then three.
'This chowder's delicious!' he chuckled with glee.
He carried on slurping the stuff in the pot
till he'd guzzled it all –

– yes, the whole blooming lot.

He'd just drunk a PINT of the Puss-Pep-Up brew.
Now what would happen?
What would that brew do?

Dad gave a big

BURP!

and declared, 'This is weird!'

'I seem to be sprouting a gingery beard!'

Then he gasped as his hands became glomping great paws, and his fingernails turned into needle-sharp claws!

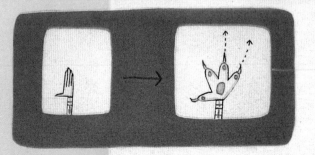

He started to quiver.
He started to quail.
Then out of the back of his
pants popped –

a tail!
That potion was potent,
no doubt about that.
My dad had turned into a gigantic...

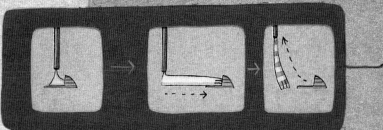

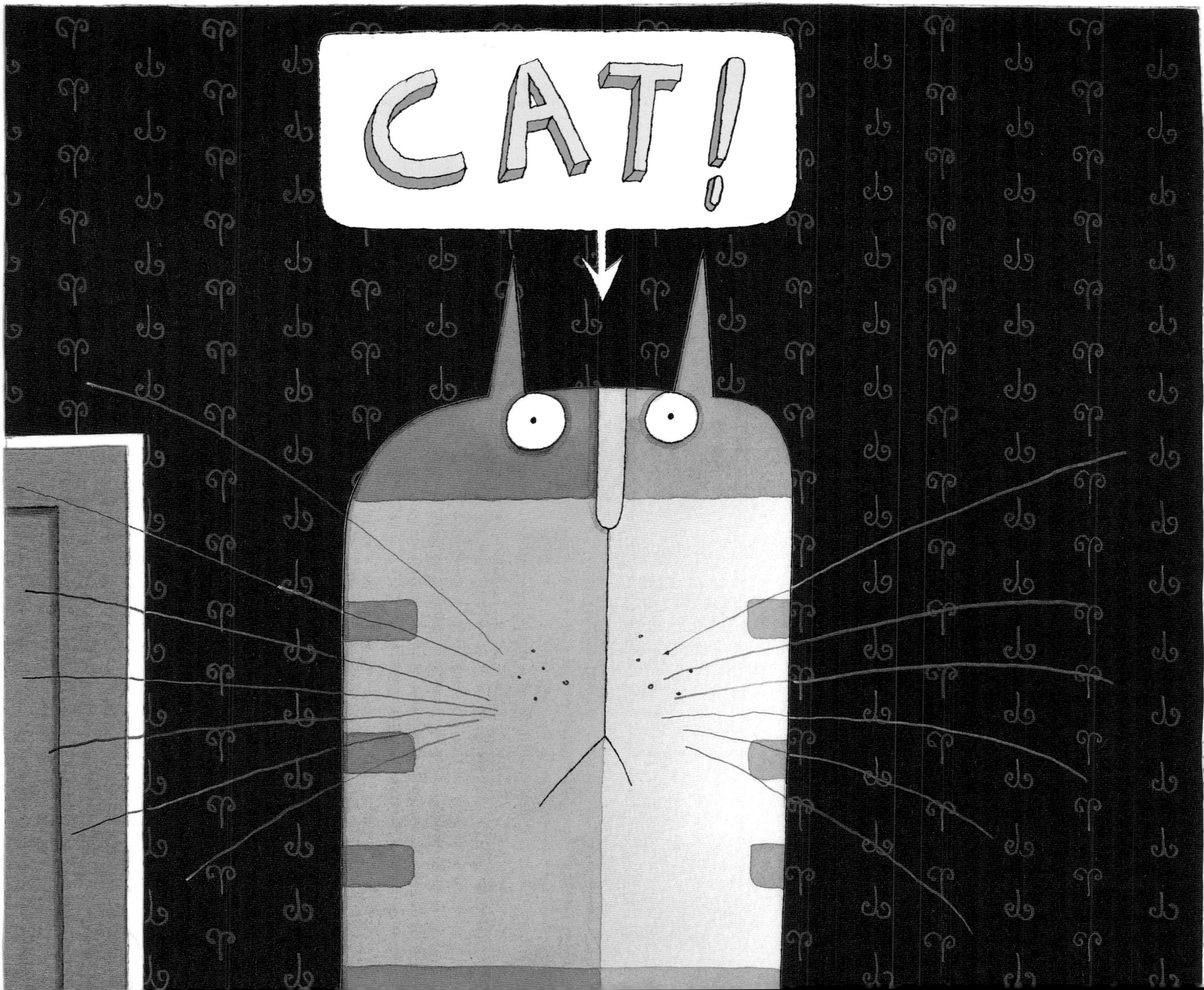
CAT!

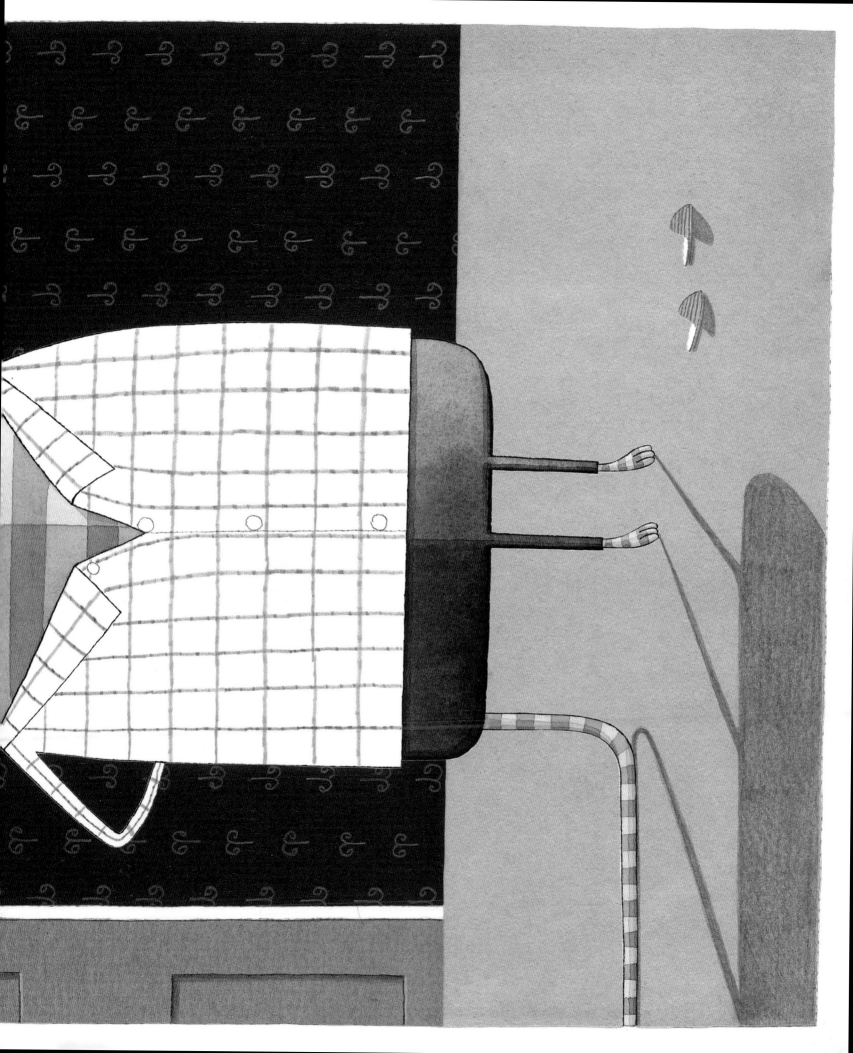

Dad sharpened his claws

on the dining room door,

and knocked our best crockery onto the floor!

He pounced on –

and swallowed –

a
very
large
bug,

and
totally
trashed
our new table and rug.

He licked himself clean with a satisfied purr.

Then –

– coughed up a large ball of fur.

He trampled the blooms
of our neighbour, Miss Hawn,
and I just can't describe
what he left on her lawn . . .

poo

Miss Hawn shouted, 'Shoo!'
from her kitchen, then . . .

Yikes!

Out of the door shot her
puppy-dog, Sikes!

Mum tried to grab him but
stumbled and tripped —

and in the kerfuffle
her bottom got nipped!

Dad hissed and spat with his hackles right up —

then fled up a tree from the fearsome wee pup.

'Stop!' we all yelled,

but we watched in dismay
as Dad reached the treetop . . .

Yip!

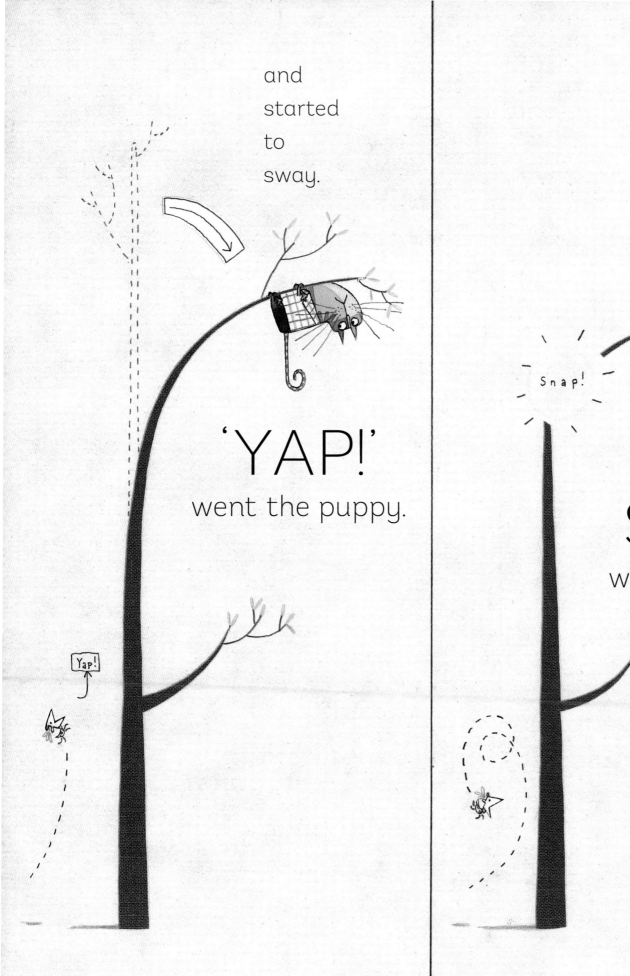

'GOSH!' we all gasped. as my Dad went

miaaaaaoooooooo

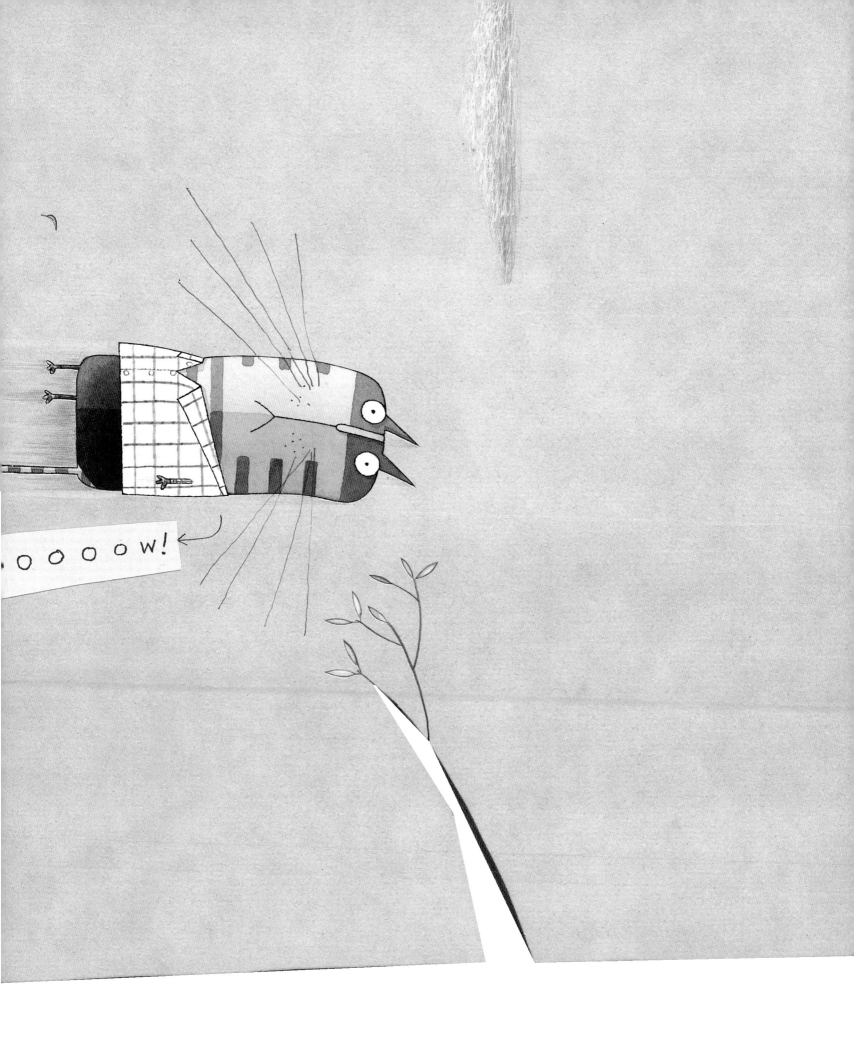

He fell in the rubbish.
What clatter and din!

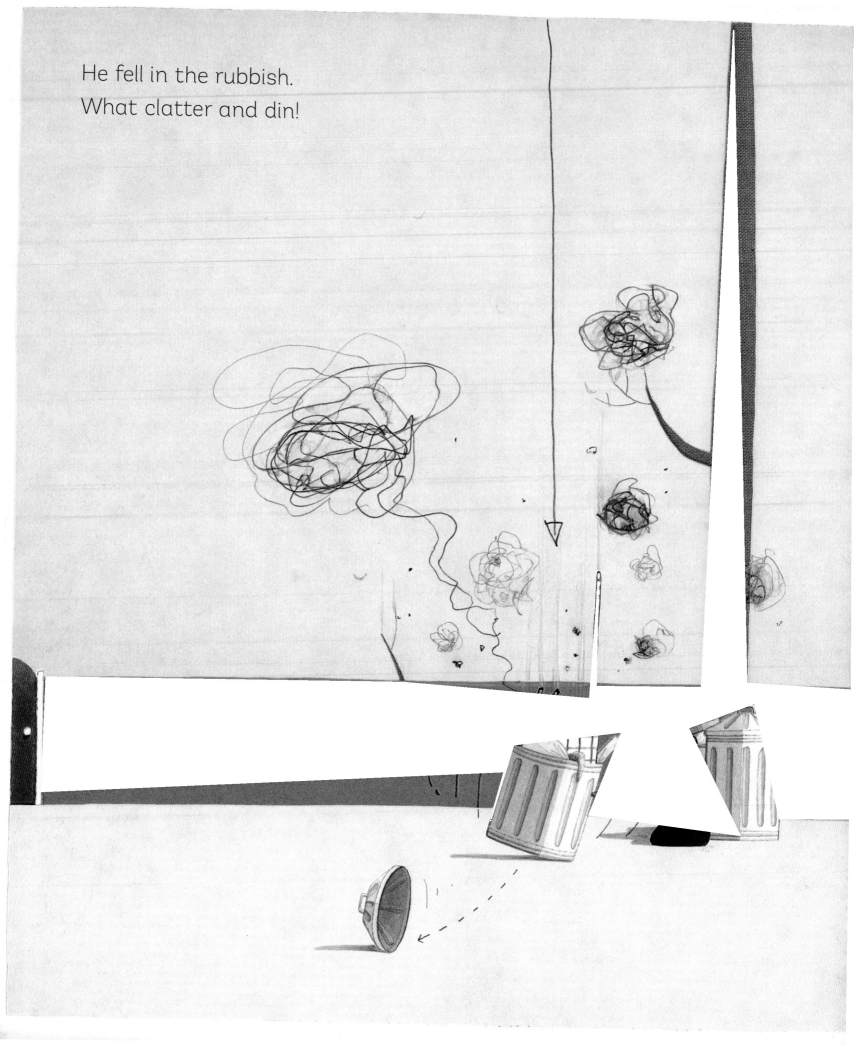

Then we heard a loud **BURP!** coming out of the bin.

Dad had
changed back
again,
quick as a flash,

and stood, quite bewildered,
in yesterday's trash.

'What happened?' he groaned.
'Am I dreaming? Or mad?'

'No,' declared Mum.

'Just
a
REAL
Dustbin
Dad.'

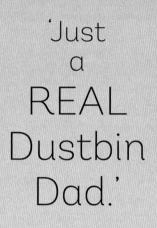

So, **never** leave food where your father can grab it.
He's likely to start up a scrap-eating habit.

Then he, too, might suffer a similar fate–

unless you eat ALL of the food on your plate!